Royal Rivals

Dennis Reymond

Contents

Glimpse of Royal blood   1

Prologue - The Origin (Lion)   4

Prologue 2 - The Origin (Tigress)   11

Chapter 1 - Dasya the cheetah   20

Chapter 2 - Saving the princess   25

Chapter 3 - For you   38

Important (read this first)   51

Chapter 4 - The Royal celebration   52

Chapter 5 - I love you for thousand times   63

Chapter 6 - Consequences   76

Glimpse of Royal blood

"Har kisi ko nahi milta, yaha pyar zindagi mei" he hummed a tune as the hot water cascaded over him and the radio playing softly in background.

He closed his eyes, lost in the music, feeling the rhythm wash away the stains of the day.

After a while, he turned off the water, the last notes of the song fading into the silence of the room. He reached for the towel, wrapping it around his waist. Droplets clung to his wet hair as he stepped out of the bathroom.

And there, in the dimly lit bedroom, lay the grotesque tableau. Lifeless bodies sprawled in awkward positions, their eyes staring into nothingness. Blood painted the walls and floor in macabre patterns. The room reeked of death.

Oddly, he didn't flinch, didn't gasp in horror. He simply stood there, towel in hand. Because it was done by him.

"Pyar chodh de, tumlogo ka zindagi hi nahi raha" he laughed mockingly at those dead bodies.

With the towel hung around his neck, he walked towards the balcony, a glass of crimson wine in his hand. The night air was filled with tension, punctuated by the staccato bursts of gunfire and the screams of the dying. Dhantara city had become a battleground, a theater of chaos where the rules of law held no sway.

He leaned against the railing, his gaze fixed on the gang war which was planned by him. It was a symphony of violence, a dance of death.

Sipping his wine, he watched as lives were extinguished with every pull of a trigger. There was an eerie satisfaction in the chaos, he felt alive amidst the death, as if the violence below was the only thing that could pierce the numbness that had consumed him.

"Sab marjao yaar, kisi ko zinda rehna nahi chahiye. Sab ekdusre ko goli maardo phir mai passport leke Japan jaunga" he shouted aggressively, the words echoing against the backdrop of violence.

But then, a sudden interruption. "Boss, she arrived" his bodyguard's voice sliced through the air. He turned, his eyes falling upon the loyal guard, bloodstains marring the fabric of his clothes.

He didn't seem worried about the situation, he gazed back at the brutal environment outside of balcony. "Toh isme Mai kya kar sakta hoo?" he took a sip from wine after questioning.

His guard began, "We need your ord-"

But before he could finish, a deafening gunshot pierced the air.

He looked back and found his guard sprawled lifeless on the ground.

Behind the lifeless body of his guard stood a lady, draped in a black dress, her fingers wrapped around a gleaming pistol. The weapon was pointed squarely at him, its cold metal a stark contrast to the heat of the moment.

Despite the dire situation, he chuckled. "Didn't expect you to teleport here suddenly," he remarked, his voice dripping with sarcasm.

"Didn't expect you to be the monster either," she said softly.

He met her gaze, unyielding. "You knew it but didn't want to believe it," he replied, his words heavy with a bitter truth.

"Toh bolo, kitna pyar karte ho tum mujhse?" she asked in a dark serious tone, her aim was pointed towards his chest.

He didn't reply immediately, instead he gazed at her. His eyes filled with sadness and his silence stretching into a heavy pause.

Then, unexpectedly a tear escaped his eyes, tracing a path down his cheek. "Pyar ke liye jitna khoon bahaya usse zyada pyar kiya."

"Goodbye Rudra" In that instant, she closed her eyes and pulled the trigger.

Prologue – The Origin (Lion)

"**S**aare auratein kaha hai!? bacchiya kaha hai??!" Daksh Verma roared. His reputation as the leader of a ruthless human trafficking syndicate was well-known, a name whispered in terror across villages. For years, he had haunted these remote hamlets, abducting innocent girls and women, destined for a life of unspeakable suffering in Syria.

This time he came here for this same reason but there was no sign of his victims, no terrified faces to greet him. Instead, there were only the crumbling ruins and the relentless flames burning the huts.

"What if they escaped from here already?" one of his guard informed with nervousness.

Daksh Verma's eyes narrowed. "Ran away, you say?" He sneered, his voice dripping with contempt. "Those girls are like caged birds, and I am their keeper." He paused, his mind racing to salvage his plan.

"Hmm, maybe. We will find girls in Haryana," Daksh declared, determination burning in his eyes.

The guard dared to voice his concerns once more, his voice shaking, "but sir Haryana mei ladkiya exist nahi karte aur west bengal mei ladkiya black magic karti hai. Rajasthan is the best option."

Daksh Verma's lips curled in distaste at the mention of Rajasthan's scorching heat. "Nah bhai, Mai nahi kar raha waha pe kaam. Bohot garmiya hai aur paani nahi milta waha. Ruk Mai thora ghum ke aata hoo."

With a predatory grace, he turned away from the smoldering ruins and strode purposefully towards the looming forest, disappearing into the shadows like a malevolent ghost.

After walking for a while through dark forest with leaves, air filled with owl's hooting. He heard a weeping sound from distance.

Daksh Verma's eyes lit up with a sinister gleam as he heard the weeping voice from the bushes. Excitement surged through him like a dark pulse, and he swiftly ran towards the source of the sound. There, amidst the tangled foliage, he found a trembling girl, her tear-streaked face framed by a yellow skirt that was now stained with dirt and despair.

A twisted smile crept across Daksh's face, his predatory instincts honed in on the vulnerable prey before him.

But before she could take more than a step, Daksh Verma's iron grip closed around her hair, yanking her back with a cruel force. With a gut-wrenching thud, she was pinned against a gnarled tree, her gasp of terror trapped in her throat.

In a brutal motion, Daksh Verma pulled the girl closer, her gasp of pain drowned out by the sound of her body slamming against the unforgiving ground.

Daksh Verma, kneeled down in front of the girl, effectively blocking her path to escape.

His eyes, cold and merciless, bore into hers, extinguishing any flicker of hope that remained within her. Trapped and defenseless, she stared back, paralyzed by fear, as the cruel reality of her situation became painfully clear.

Slowly he started unbuckling his belt faster, excitement and evil smirk was visible in his face. He didn't care about her cry, scream, pain. All he wanted was to take away her soul and crush it into pieces.

But suddenly a searing pain erupted in Daksh Verma's face, and his eyes widened in shock as a sharp, excruciating sensation coursed through him. Blood began to flow profusely, staining his cruel features. With a horrified gasp, he looked down towards the source of his torment and saw a gleaming knife thrust through the area of his throat, its blade slick with his own blood.

He was struggling to speak against the pain until another merciless slash given to him which silenced Daksh Verma forever.

The blade, sharp and unforgiving, pierced through his skull, ending his reign of terror in an instant. His lifeless body crumpled to the forest floor.

The moonlight revealed the teenage boy standing behind Daksh, his dark, messy hair clinging to his sweat-soaked forehead. His t-shirt, once vibrant, was now stained with the blood of their tormentor. In his eyes, there was a mix of anger and pain.

With a trembling hand, the teenage boy reached out towards the girl, his fingers stained with the blood of Daksh.

Tears welled up in her eyes as she recognized the teenage boy before her. "Rudrajeet?" she whispered, disbelief and relief intertwining in her voice. "You here?" she asked, her grip on his hand tightening as he helped her to her feet.

"Yes, it's me, Taniya," Rudrajeet whispered, his voice choked with emotion. Tears welled up again in Taniya's eyes as she realized that her savior was none other than her younger brother.

"Rudra...you killed someone" she said, still in shock of what she witnessed. Her wide eyes gazing at Daksh's dead body.

Rudra cupped her cheeks gently, his eyes locked onto hers. "Tum meei behen ho, aur meri behen ko jab koi apmaan karega toh usko jeene nahi dunga shaanti se aur agar woh meri behen par haath uthayega toh..." he groaned in anger. "TOH USKA GARDAN KAAT KE USKE HAATH MEI DEDUNGA"

She was terrified to see her brother's rage, Rudrajeet was always hot headed child but she never expected this kind of rage from him.

"Now what...Rudra?" she asked, worrying about their future fate.

"His guards will come here soon, searching for him," he said with urgent tone. He held up a container of petrol.

"Sister, let's put petrol around him," he pointed to the lifeless body of Daksh, "and when they come here, just burn them into ashes."

Her voice quivered with fear and reason as she protested against her brother's horrifying plan. "But this whole forest will burn into ashes, we can't do that," she said, her eyes wide with horror at the thought of the entire landscape being consumed by flames.

"Tumhare liye pura duniya jala dunga behen, tumhare liye kuch bhi karunga" Rudrajeet said, his voice tinged with an eerie intensity. In that moment, it was clear that he was willing to go to any length to protect his sibling, even if it meant embracing darkness.

She just nodded, have no choice but to agree with her brother's sinister plan.

In the eerie glow of the moonlight, both siblings began to pour petrol around Daksh's lifeless body, her hands shaking with fear but Rudrajeet's hand didn't. Instead, his hand was steady with confidence.

Silently, they lined the trail of petrol leading from Daksh's body to the edge of the forest, setting the stage for their grim plan. The scent of petrol hung heavy in the air, mingling with the natural aroma of the woods.

Minutes later when they were waiting outside of forest, he heard fearful scream of Daksh's guards. Rudra realized they had discovered dead body of Daksh. Without a moment's hesitation, he swiftly lit a matchstick and hurled it towards the petrol-soaked ground. The flame caught the volatile liquid, igniting a fierce line that raced toward the center of the forest.

The night erupted in a blaze of fire, the forest becoming an inferno of destruction. The guards' screams intensified, but Rudrajeet's expression remained calm. He watched with confident eyes as the flames consumed them, their cries mixing with the crackling of the fire.

"Rudra..." Rudrajeet turned to his sister's voice, both holding hands of each other. "What now?" she questioned him, "what will we do now..."

"What will we do now...this question hit me harder, but I knew the answer"

Rudrajeet hugged his sister tightly, she buried her face into his chest. "Next time, we won't kill these monsters. I'll be powerful enough to control these monsters under my feet."

"It was my ultimate goal, be powerful more than anyone. This is why, we both went to Bombay in illegal way. After we managed to reach there, I didn't know from where to start our journey

I was clueless. So I randomly started working in small restaurants, washing their dishes, I didn't let my sister do anything. I used to get 10₹ per week but I managed to feed her even though I had to lie to her that I've eaten but in reality I was starving.

One day I ended up in street fight with local gangster but in fight, I overpowered him. Unfortunately he was one of the member of Bombay's biggest mafia Haji Mastaan. I thought it was end of us, I was regretting for first time, we had nowhere to go now.

But fate had other plans, Haji mastaan was impressed from me and he hired me as their gang member. I used to deliver drugs. Trust me, it was most easiest work for me and I enjoyed it alot. Imagine fooling polices and delivering products worth crores.

I worked there for 7 months until Haji motherfucker fucked me up. He ordered me to do robbery in bank at night, he promised me that he'll pay me 1 lakh₹ and I succeeded in that task but police surrounded the whole bank, waiting to arrest me.

I realized this was plan of Haji, he didn't need me anymore so he set up this plan to trap me. Sadly, I betrayed my own work partners to escape from there. I quickly ran to my sister after my escape, best thing was I escaped with bag full of money.

If someone fucks me up, I fuck them from everywhere, that's why I revealed some information to his rival 'Dawood Ibrahim' and this thing led to huge gang war in Bombay.

With the stolen money and Dawood's huge reward for my help, my sister and I went to city name 'Dhantara'. I invested my money in business to open a shop, but at night my efforts used to go in dirty businesses.

Whoever stood infront of me as obstacles, I performed a perfect murder to silence them. Soon, I was close to get the royal life, filled with power and luxury. The era of royalty in my city 'Dhantara'

To be continued

Prologue 2 - The Origin (Tigress)

"Yeh kamini kaha hai?" said Rahul angrily. He was a spoiled student of Dhantara International School, known for his reckless behavior and disregard for rules. His father's position as a close associate of the Chief Minister had only fueled his arrogance, leading him down a path of entitlement and misuse of power.

Right now he stood in center of fight club arena, surrounded by a raucous crowd.

"Oye jhaatu!" Rahul's heart leaped as he heard that familiar voice calling out to him. He turned in the direction of the voice and saw a girl making her way through the crowd.

She moved with a confidence that demanded attention, paying no heed to the curious or bewildered faces around her.

As she finally reached the edge of the arena, her gaze locked onto Rahul's. With a self-assured tone, she declared, "aagayi mai"

She threw away her jacket, confidently positioning herself at the opposite side of arena, facing Rahul.

Rahul always had crush on her, proposed her for dates many times but everytime he recieved rejection from her. After he got to know she is best student of martial art class, he challenged her for duo in fight club and if she loses then she'll date him for months.

Rahul, driven by his desperate desire to win her over, reminded her "if you lose then you'll date me for four months."

The girl, unyielding and poised, met Rahul's challenge head-on. With a steely resolve in her eyes, she accepted, "You're on."

In a lightning-fast exchange, He rushed at her. Rahul's punch sliced through the air, but the girl's reflexes were quicker. She deftly moved her head, narrowly avoiding the blow. Before Rahul could adjust, he aimed a swift kick, but she gracefully flipped backward, out of harm's way.

As she landed, her movements were fluid and controlled. In a strategic move, she slid her leg along the floor, sweeping Rahul's feet out from under him. With a resounding thud, Rahul hit the ground, pain shooting through his body.

The tension in the arena reached a crescendo as the girl launched a powerful punch aimed at Rahul's face. With a swift, practiced motion, Rahul rolled back, narrowly evading the blow. The spectators gasped, impressed by his agility and quick thinking.

Seizing the opportunity, Rahul countered with a flying kick, his determination evident in his every move. However, the girl, displaying remarkable finesse, dodged his attack in a stylish and effortless manner. Her movements were like a dance, a mesmerizing display of skill and grace that left the crowd in awe.

Rahul got fueled with frustration and anger. He unleashed a flurry of punches and kicks, his movements becoming increasingly erratic and aggressive. However, the girl seemed to anticipate his every move with uncanny precision. Swiftly and effortlessly, she dodged his blows, her movements graceful and controlled.

"FUCK YOU!" Exhausted and gasping for breath, Rahul lowered his guard, his chest heaving with the effort he had put into the fight. As he looked up, searching for his opponent, he realized she was nowhere to be seen. Confusion flickered in his eyes, and in that moment of vulnerability, he made the mistake of turning around.

In a lightning-fast movement, before he could react, he felt a sudden impact on his jaw. The force of the kick sent shockwaves of pain through his body, and he staggered, his vision momentarily blurring.

The girl had reappeared behind him, her swift and precise strike catching him completely off guard.

The crowd gasped in astonishment at her unexpected move.

As Rahul lay on the floor, blood trickling from his mouth, the sound of a bell rang out through the arena, signaling the end of the match.

She stood tall, a triumphant smirk on her face, her pride evident in every step she took. The spectators erupted into a mix of cheers and stunned murmurs.

Rahul slowly pulled himself up from the floor, his pride wounded and his spirit crushed.

The girl looked at him with a confident smirk, her words cutting through the air. "Better luck next time," she said, her tone laced with attitude.

"Next time phirse try karenge" Rahul extended his hand for a handshake, However, the girl simply shook her head and replied, "Mereko nahi lagta ki phirse try karneka mauka milegi mujhe."

Before Rahul could voice his confusion, she moved swiftly. With lightning speed, she twisted his hand and delivered three powerful punches. The blows came fast and hard, leaving Rahul disoriented and defenseless. To add a final blow, she kicked him in the most vulnerable spot and then slapped his face with a sharp, stinging impact.

The force of her actions left Rahul unconscious, sprawled on the floor.

"Arre chutiye, tere khara hone ka laayak tak nahi dungi toh mauka kaise milega. Tharki sala" she spat at him after cursing him.

With Rahul defeated and unconscious, the girl walked away, her head held high.

"MISS NAVISHA!!!" she heard a familiar voice from distant and source of voice was getting louder in every seconds. Her heart skipped a bit as she realized to whom this voice belongs.

It was voice of her father's right hand Vihaan.

He pushed through the crowd and came towards her. "Kya kar rahi ho aap yaha?" he asked with worries on face.

Navisha's eyes narrowed with annoyance of his clingy behavior and uncomfortable sound of crowd.

A person busted inside of fight club with a sudden announcement which sent shockwave through the crowd. Panic ensured as the words "POLICE FORCE IS HERE FOR RAID" reverberated through the air. People scattered in all directions, desperate to escape the impending raid.

"Jaldi miss, mere saath chaliye warna musibaat hosakta hai" Vihaan out-stretched his hand. She tightly grasped the hand of him and they sprinted together towards the back gate, weaving through the fleeing crowd.

Navisha and Vihaan managed to reach the car waiting at the back gate. With a quick exchange of glances, jumped into the car and sped away, leaving behind the chaotic scene.

"So, miss, tell me what were you doing in there?" her father's right-hand man asked, his voice stern, while he drove.

"I was just chilling," Navi said nonchalantly, trying to downplay the situation.

"That's not a place to chill," he admonished, his tone firm. "I know your idea of chilling extends from theaters to libraries, cafes, and gaming zones. Not this disgusting place."

Vihaan glared at Navisha, his anger palpable. "Your father will screw both of us if he gets to know this," he said frustratingly.

Navisha's eyes widened with urgency. "Crazy, but please don't tell this to father. That's how we both will be safe, I promise this is the last time," she pleaded.

"Fine, but you need to make sure this truly is the last time, miss Navi. Your father's trust is not something to be taken lightly," he warned, his tone stern.

Navisha nodded.

Navisha and her father, Aditya, stood on the balcony of their high-rise apartment, gazing out at the breathtaking cityscape that stretched out before them. The twinkling lights of the skyscrapers painted a mesmerizing picture against the night sky.

"I truly miss my cousin," Navisha said, her voice soft and melancholic. "Wish he was here."

Aditya placed a comforting hand on her shoulder and turned to look at her. "I understand, girl. We all do," he replied, his tone filled with empathy.

"Aaj raat mujhe ek important chiz announcement karna hai" He continued.

She turned her attention to him. "Hmm?"

"So I need you to be there for me" Aditya replied.

Navisha nodded with a smile, understanding the urgency because her father never invited her for any meeting since she's just 15 years old so getting involved in mafia world was forbidden for her.

The sudden change in her father's behavior made her curious and excited.

Together, they turned and made their way to hall room.

As they entered the hall room, a hush fell over the crowd of royal mafias. Aditya led the way, and to Navisha's surprise, applause erupted throughout the room at her arrival. Her eyes widened in astonishment, but she maintained her composure, following her father to the stage.

She was amazed by the beauty of room, the music was growing louder as she was closing her path to stage. She learned the royalty of mafia which she never witnessed due to school and private life. But tonight her father gave her chance to view their royalty.

"This truly reminds me of movie Godfather, oh my God" she thought.

As the clapping subsided, Aditya took the stage, and all eyes were on him and his daughter, Navisha.

"So, every respected member of the mafia world, I truly honor your loyalty towards me and the strength you have shared with us," Aditya's voice resonated through the microphone, commanding the attention of everyone in the room.

The whole room fell into silence with smile on every guest's face.

"Tonight, I'm gonna make a huge announcement," Aditya declared, his gaze shifting towards Navisha, who felt a rush of nerves. Her heart pounded in her chest as she awaited his words.

"From tomorrow, my daughter Navisha will be part of my business, and she will hold 40% of the profit. Everyone shall respect her, treat her accordingly, and this party is to welcome her into our mafia world," Aditya's words echoed through the room, sending a ripple of astonishment among the gathered mafia members.

Navisha couldn't believe what her father said. The mix of surpriseness and excitement washed over her face, her fear came true in this night.

"Mafia...? me...? business? abey yeh buddha mere life ke beech bohot tang karta hai. Mafia life mei involve hona matlab no Netflix, no wattpad books, no anime. Abe yaar mai chutiya hoo ki mai sperm race win kiya. ABE YAAR MAI 15 SAAL KI HOO" she was angry from inside but no one could notice it because of her fake smile. Along with being angry, she was scared of her future.

The room again buzzed into applause, the members acknowledging the significance of the moment.

That's how my life changed. I had huge argument with my father after the party ended, I asked her for this dumb announcement and reason was simple. My cousin was killed by unknown murderer and I'm smarter than anyone in family to lead the business with my dad. So he chose me, wow! brilliant.

I watched Scarface, Godfather, Goodfellas, Peaky blinders type fabulous mafia stuff so I have ideas how mafia world works. Nah don't think our mafia life will be like those wattpad books we read, they are written by teens with hormones who doesn't know M of mafias.

1 week later

Navi was engrossed in her analysis of the underworld market, listening to music while sitting on a black chair. Lost in thought, she was evaluating strategies and considering various moves for their business. However, her focus was abruptly interrupted when Vihaan approached her.

"You shall open the news," he said, his tone leaving no room for argument.

Navi nodded, acknowledging the order. She turned on the TV news.

"Good evening. In a tragic turn of events, the young Rahul Sharma who was admitted in hospital and his father came to pick him up after his discharnve, have met a devastating fate. Their car plummeted off a mountain cliff earlier today, resulting in a fatal accident. Authorities are still investigating the circumstances surrounding this heartbreaking incident."

A subtle smile played on her lips as she watched the screen.

"You did it, right?" Vihaan asked her, his voice low and filled with intrigue.

Yes I did it, he was being pain in the ass and I knew he'll tell his so called political father about me and because of this bratty richie rich my dad would face troubles. My dad was nice with his father so no one will suspect us, but I don't trust politicians. Politics are all about betrayal for benefits.

Well, I put less effort in making plan and spent more effort on finding someone to execute it. That's why I'm proud of myself

To be continued

Chapter 1 - Dasya the cheetah

"If you don't spend one night with us then you will never see your brother"

One voice call ruined her peace. Taniya had some ideas about Rudrajeet's conflicts between mexican cartels. Rudrajeet's refusal to yield to their demands for territories had ignited a fierce rivalry, a battle that transcended borders and morals.

The Mexican cartels were a ruthless force, devoid of any shred of empathy. Their brutal methods had been demonstrated when they annihilated the Cali cartels, leaving no survivors, not even children. Killed them, raped women of their family and sold them to other countries.

Now their darkness turned towards Indian mafia, Rudrajeet Ray.

Taniya clenched her fists, her mind racing as she considered the impossible choice before her. She knew that one night with the mafia would mean selling her purity. But refusing meant signing her brother's death warrant.

Taniya thought death is better than giving your body to these devils so she pulled her drawer open and took out a small glinting blade.

Her trembling hand held the blade dangerously close to her wrist.

But as fate would have it, a soft knock on her room's door startled her. The housemaid's voice broke through the thick veil of despair, "Ma'am, Rudrajeet sir is calling you for dinner. Please come, he's waiting for you."

The blade slipped from Taniya's grasp, clattering onto the floor. The world outside of mansion was turning against her happiness but her brother was waiting for her.

With shaky hands, Taniya wiped away her tears, took a deep breath, and made a decision. She would sacrifice her own innocence and pride for the sake of her brother, Rudrajeet. Because Rudrajeet had faced unimaginable hardships, enduring bullying and mistreatment from society. Despite the darkness that surrounded them, he had risen above it all, becoming strong and powerful, all for her.

☐

Somewhere in Dhantara

The large warehouse was a cavernous space, dimly lit by flickering fluorescent lights hanging from the high ceiling. The air was thick with the acrid smell of cigarettes and the pungent scent of alcohol, creating an atmosphere that felt suffocating and surreal. Crates and barrels were scattered haphazardly around the perimeter, casting long shadows in the dim light, while graffiti-covered walls hinted at the space's illicit history.

In the midst of the chaotic gathering, a makeshift table stood as a sinister centerpiece. Three ominous figures surrounded a man in his thirties, their faces twisted with cruelty. The man was forcefully kneeled down, his eyes wide with fear. His hands were bound, and his clothes were stained and torn.

The crowd's murmurs grew hushed when they saw a sudden appearance of a man with long hair, a beard, and wearing a black half-sleeve shirt.

In his hands, he carried a gleaming katana, its blade catching the dim light of the warehouse. A palpable aura of power and authority surrounded him as he approached, his steps echoing in the silence.

"All Hail Dasya!" a voice cried out, breaking the stillness, and in an instant, the entire crowd erupted into a deafening cheer. The chant echoed off the walls of the warehouse, a fervent declaration of loyalty and respect.

Dasya's approach was deliberate and unhurried as he closed the gap between himself and the man who knelt. The man's voice cracked with fear and desperation as he cried out, "DASYA! What is this? You were going to work for our brother. Why are you doing this?"

Dasya leaned forward, his eyes locked with the man's. "Paquito, Your brother is a coward. I've come to learn that he uses innocent people, particularly women, for his own amusement. Such shameful acts are something I can no longer tolerate, especially when he threatened the person I love... Taniya."

"Por favor, leave me, I apologize on his behalf" Paquito's pleas were desperate, his voice trembling with fear as he begged. "I have two children, and they're at college. I must take care of them too."

Dasya smirked, a bitter and cynical twist of his lips. "College?" he scoffed. "Your children are gone. You should have taken care of them when they harassed a college girl."

Paquito was surprised to know this truth, he started wailing for his children's death. His eyes were watered already.

"When someone messes up with something I care about, they increase my interest in being bloody sweet," Dasya declared, his voice low and chilling.

Before Paquito could say something. Dasya's men held the Paquito's trembling hand against the table. Dasya's katana slashed through the air, leaving a trail of terror in its wake.

The first slash sent shivers through the onlookers, the sound of steel meeting flesh echoing in the warehouse. Paquito's anguished scream pierced the heavy air, a stark reminder of the brutality that lurked in their world.

With swift and deliberate motions, Dasya continued his assault, each slash met with another cry of agony. Five times the blade struck, leaving the man's hand a mangled mess. Dasya paused, taking a deep breath, his eyes steely and unflinching.

In one fluid motion, Dasya swung his katana with lightning speed, severing the man's head from his body. Dasya's face got painted by Paquito's blood which splashed from body.

Dasya turned around to crowd with blazing gaze, Paquito's blood dropping from his face.

"HAMARE PAAS 24 GHANTE HAI! 24 GHANTE KE ANDAR HUM PURE MEXICAN CARTEL KO KHATAM KARDENGE" he thundered. "ABHI RAAT 12 BAJA HAI AUR KAL RAAT TAK KA TIME HAI HAMARE PAAS"

The crowd absorbed his words with excitement, knowing that the coming 24 hours would be a whirlwind of violence and chaos.

His guard approached with a large bag, and Dasya seized it, the jingle of cash filling the air as he unzipped the chain. With a swift motion, he dropped a substantial amount of money onto the table, his eyes gleaming with ruthless resolve. "Khatam kardo unke supporters ko, chahe koi bhi ho. Police ho ya judge ho, politician ho ya mafia ho. Jaha pe bhi chupe ho, dhund dhund ke maaro unko. Jo karpayega, uska life settlement kiya jayega"

The warehouse erupted in a deafening uproar as Dasya's followers roared their allegiance. Dasya's command had set them in motion, and the adrenaline coursed through their veins as they prepared to carry out his ruthless directive.

"YOUR TIME STARTS NOW!" Dasya's voice boomed, setting the crowd into motion.

Without a moment's hesitation, everyone in the warehouse surged towards the room situated at the left corner. Inside, a chilling array of weapons lay strewn across multiple desks – choppers, blades, guns, hammers, and an array of instruments designed for destruction. Each person grabbed a weapon of their choice. Excitement etched in their face.

With their weapons in hand, Dasya's army stormed out of the warehouse, their footsteps thundering on the pavement as they scattered in different directions, their hearts consumed by a single mission.

To execute those who are related to mexican cartels without any mercy.

To be continued

A/N :- finally chapter 1 is here. Thanks for giving my book a try, please drop your views about this chapter.

Also your opinion on Dasya's character.

Chapter 2 - Saving the princess

"You have strong guards around you, luxurious life, protective brother but still you're helpless. Pathetic, right? That's what I feel, pathetic and helpless. My body shivers after thinking what will happen tonight with me. But I'm doing it, for Rudra...I love my brother more than anything" Taniya's face was numb when she penned down her sadness onto the small diary in the room decorated by statues of animals, book shelves.

She stood up, closing her diary and walked outside with money bag clutched in her hand. Her eyes fell upon the imposing Ganesha temple nestled in the corner of hall.

Feeling a deep connection to her faith, Taniya bowed down in silent prayer, her lips moving in fervent whispers. She sought strength from the divine God.

She pulled out a flower from her bag and put it on the Golden plate placed near the feet of Ganesha and raised her head. With a final glance, she turned around to exit door.

"Ma'am, shall I inform Rudrajeet sir?" the guard asked her.

Taniya replied gently. "Tell him that I'm out with my friends and I'll be back in evening."

The guard, respecting Taniya's decision, nodded in acknowledgment. "Understood, ma'am. I'll convey the message to Rudrajeet sir." With that, he stepped back, allowing Taniya to continue her journey.

□

"Why the hell my brother is not picking up my phone?" Pedro, the Mexican drug cartel exclaimed, he was circling around the lavish room. Rich mahogany furniture adorned with intricate carvings filled the space and walls were covered by tapestries depicting scenes of brutality.

A grand fireplace stood at the side.

His Indian uncle on the wheelchair remained silent, his eyes sharp and observant, as if he too sensed the brewing storm that threatened their empire because according to them unanswered calls meant trouble.

Pedro's frustration deepened as few guards hurriedly entered the room with news. "Sir, our exporters aren't picking up any calls. There are no updates about our stocks. We tried to call our bribed police officer, but he's not answering. Something is wrong."

Pedro's jaw clenched as he processed the guards' report. "Send someone to the exporters' location immediately. I don't care how, but find them and get updates. And make sure our police contact gets our message. We can't afford any delays," he commanded, his voice seething with urgency.

The guard hesitated for a moment before responding, "Sir, we're having difficulty tracing the exporter's location at the moment. It might take some time."

Pedro's patience wore thin, and with a swift, furious motion, he smashed the horse statue on the table, causing his guards to flinch. "No excuses. Find them," he growled.

Realizing the gravity of the situation, the guards nodded fervently. "Yes, sir. We'll do everything in our power to locate them."

"Good. Alert our mafia partners immediately. Gather all our men and bring them to the mansion," Pedro ordered, his voice firm. "We need to fortify our defenses and be prepared for whatever comes our way."

The guards wasted no time and hurriedly left the room, their footsteps echoing down the corridor as they carried out Pedro's commands.

Pedro's thoughts were interrupted by a notification sound from mobile. He unlocked the mobile and opened whatsapp, an unknown number had around 16 messages in chats.

He opened the chat curiously but what he saw was unbelievable. His hand started trembling as he saw the images in chat.

His eyes widened in horror at the gruesome images that flooded the screen—his supporters, once loyal and fierce, now lay lifeless in a pool of blood. Some were mutilated, their limbs missing, while others bore the cruel mark of bullets and sharp blades. The room seemed to spin around him as he stared at the nightmarish scenes, his breath caught in his throat.

His shakingly hand dropped the phone, the sound of its impact on the floor echoing through the room.

Before Pedro could process what happened, an explosive sound echoed through the room.

Pedro didn't take any seconds to rush towards the window. He slid the curtain aside to witness what happened.

His eyes widened as he saw massive explosion outside their gates. His fleet of cars lay in ruins, engulfed in flames and billowing smoke that cloaked the surroundings in an eerie, foggy haze.

In the haze of smoke, Dasya and his men emerged. They were armed with assault rifles except Dasya who was carrying his sharp katana, ready to slash anyone.

"Fire these bloody mexicans" Dasya commanded.

Following his command, they opened fire on Pedro's guards. Desperation filled the air as Pedro's guards scrambled for cover, but the onslaught was relentless. Many fell, their lives brutally snuffed out in the hail of bullets.

In the middle of chaos, Dasya was stepping forward, his path focused on huge main door located few meters away, in front of him.

"Dasya..." Pedro uttered his name in shock.

His Indian uncle spoke "Dasya? I thought it was Rudrajeet"

Pedro looked at his uncle, his face was wet by sweat already.

"Ab agar Dasya yaha aaraha hai toh" his uncle continued. "Toh sala shaitan bhi ghabra jayega"

Dasya was few steps away from main door, one of his men released a rocket from missile launcher, blasting main door.

The force of the explosion sent the door flying inward, splintering it into a rain of debris. Without hesitation, Dasya rushed inside, his katana gleaming in the chaos.

Dasya's katana became blur of steel when it was cutting through air while being engaged into fight with Pedro's guards.His movements were fluid and lethal, a dance of death that left no room for escape.

In the dire moment Dasya found himself surrounded by four men wielding sledgehammers and choppers.

Behind him, another assailant aimed a rifle directly at his head.

Dasya made his move quickly, his threwkatana with unparalleled accuracy. The blade flew through the air and struck in the rifle-armed assailant's chest. The man collapsed, his grip on the rifle loosening as he fell.

In the same heartbeat, the other four attackers rushed at Dasya, their weapons raised high.

Dasya dodged the swing of the chopper.Seizing the opportunity, he delivered a powerful punch to his assailant's face, the impact sending the man staggering backward, dazed and disoriented.

Another assailant swung a sledgehammer with brutal force. He gracefully lowered himself to the ground, sliding to the side just in time to avoid the deadly blow. Dasya capitalized on the opportunity, delivering a powerful kick to the man's back.

Dasya moved away from him for taking a moment to breath but suddenly his hands were grabbed by 4th person.

Dasya started struggling to release himself but he was overpowered by the person. The chopper-wielding assailant walked menacingly, ready to strike at Dasya's throat.

He planted his feet firmly on the fourth person's leg, leveraging the unexpected support to break free from the grip. The person released Dasya.

Seizing the opportunity, Dasya propelled the person forward, his body colliding with the path of the chopper guy's swing.

In a horrifying twist, the chopper guy's blade unintentionally, sliced through the fourth person's throat. Blood erupted from the wound, splattering the flood in a gruesome display.

The chopper holding person's mind got consumed by murderous rage, he swung his blade in desperation to kill Dasya.

Dasya quickly scanned the area for available advantage. His eyes locked onto a nearby flower pot, and without hesitation, he grabbed it and smashed it forcefully against the assailant's head.

The assailant fell down. Dasya took the chance, grabbing him and slamming him against the ground.

Dasya shouted in rage and began throwing blows of punches.

After few hard punches, his eyes fell on the chopper. Dasya picked it up to end the downed assailant but he sensed another danger from behind. Dasya swung the chopper backward.

The force of the blow sliced through the flesh, causing the attacker to cry out in agony. He stumbled forward, losing his balance and control over the sledgehammer. With a loud crash, the heavy weapon fell to the floor,

The fallen attacker grasped Dasya's hand, his fingers curling around the chopper's handle. Dasya wrapped his legs around the person's neck, pinning him forcefully against the ground and slamming him against the floor once again.

Taking advantage of the opening, Dasya stood up and grabbed the sledgehammer guy's collar, his grip firm and unyielding.

Dasya hurled the sledgehammer guy to the other side of the room. The attacker crashed into a wall, the impact leaving him momentarily stunned.

Dasya lifted up the fallen hammer from the ground and unleashed a savage blow upon the already wounded assailant's legs, breaking them with a sickening crunch.

Undeterred by the cries of pain, Dasya raised the sledgehammer once more, his heart pounding with determination. By a single, forceful swing, he brought the heavy hammer down, smashing the assailant's head.

The chopper guy surged forward, Dasya, quick on his feet, attempted to evade the attack, but he stumbled and fell to the ground due to the presence of the dead body of the first person who had held the rifle.

Dasya's hand found the rifle. With a rapid pull of the trigger, he shot the rushing assailant in the stomach. The impact halted the chopper guy's charge, his momentum disrupted by the searing pain.

Taking the moment, Dasya pulled out his katana and sliced the attacker's hand. The chopper clattering on ground.

Dasya smirked "kya hua re kutte? Bohot chilla raha tha." After finishing his sentence, Dasya swung the blade around his body. Lining the wounds on his back and front. The guy kneeled down on ground, still alive and taking breath.

Dasya pushed the katana deep into his stomach and pulled it out. The attacker fell down, lifeless.

Dasya continued moving into the mansion, until then his followers got inside with him and all started shooting with their guns. Shattering expensive artifacts and furnitures, killing Pedro's men.

□

"I'm not going to die" Dasya muttered to himself. He gathered cash and drugs, shoving them into the heavy bag. Ready to abandon his empire and escape.

A thud sound echoed loudly and the entrance door got violently opened by Dasya. Holding the katana, Dasya stood before him. Bloodied face, cold eyes gazing into Pedro's soul.

"If Lionel notice this, he will crush you! don't think you can do what your brother did Dasya. LIONEL WILL KILL YOU!!" Pedro's voice thundered with warning.

Dasya didn't show any emotions, he moved forward with katana.

Pedro cried out. "Leave me alone Dasya! I swear, if he gets to know what you did and who are you. He won't let you live pea-"

Dasya ended his life by 1 slash of katana, not letting Pedro finish what he said. Dasya wiped the blood from katana with a towel laying on sofa. "Lionel jab ayega dekha jayega, Dhantara abhi bhi Rudrajeet ka hai."

□

As the evening descended, Taniya stood at a few distance away from Pedro's mansion. She was feeling her heart being shattered. Then a car pulled up before her. She expected it to be Pedro's car but unexpectedly the driver was Dasya.

"Dasya...you?" she stammered, surprise and confusion etched on her face.

"Zyada confuse mat ho, Dasya ne sab theek kardiya" he said softly and winked at her. "Ab Rudrajeet sir ke paas chal, Mai tujhe pohochadeta."

Taniya nodded. She got inside the car and settled into the backseat. Dasya skillfully maneuvered the vehicle away from the scene and driving them toward Rudrajeet's mansion.

Dasya said. "Tune dopahar se kuch khaya nahi hoga na?". He picked up a cup of ice cream and offered it to Taniya. "Baad mei tereko Vada pav, pani puri khiladeta hoo. Abhi chips khaale"

Taniya smiled, accepting the ice cream. As she opened the cover of cup and stuffed ice cream into her mouth. She said "thanks alot Dasya"

Dasya's cheeks tinged with a faint blush at Taniya's gratitude. He smiled warmly and replied, "No problem, always at your service."

"By the way, how did you know about I'm starving and about my problem? I didn't even tell this to my own brother" she raised a question.

Dasya calmly replied. "I'm stalking you" he confessed. "wait- it's not like I was breaking your privacy. I'm not that creepy, it's just I like you and I just check on you sometimes... I don't like you, I love you"

She didn't say anything for a moment which made Dasya nervous but the silence broke by her sweet laugh. Dasya was in love with her when he saw her during their teen age and after he came back to Dhantara from London, he was checking on her.

"Oh really? then you have to talk to my brother first before we date. I never accepted anyone's proposal because of Rudra and you know. No one proposed to me except 2 or 3 college mates" She stated.

"That's what I'm gonna do" Dasya unhesitatingly confirmed.

"AYO WHAT-" Taniya exclaimed, she hadn't expect Dasya to follow her request this quickly.

▢

Rudrajeet was sitting on his grand golden chair, his guards standing vigilantly in the corners of the room. When Taniya walked into the mansion, a genuine smile broke across his face. He couldn't contain his emotions and rushed toward her, enveloping her in a tight and heartfelt hug.

It's too late, why did you lie about where you went? I was worried," Rudrajeet teared up. Taniya patted his back. "I'm okay Rudra...don't worry, I'm sorry for making you worry."

Rudrajeet wiped his tears and curiously asked Taniga who had brought her safely. Her gaze shifted to Dasya.

Dasya stepped forward, bowing down with respect. "I'm Dasya Kumar, I've brought her safely with no scratches."

"Taniya, sweetheart, I'm glad you're back safe," Rudrajeet began, his voice softening with concern. "But I need to talk to Dasya privately for a moment. Could you please go to your room?"

Taniya met her brother's eyes, She nodded with trust. "Of course, Rudra. I'll be in my room if you need me."

With a warm and reassuring pat on her shoulder, she turned and made her way to her room.

Rudrajeet gestured towards Dasya, indicating for him to follow. Dasya nodded and followed Rudrajeet to office within the mansion.

Through the path, Dasya saw many workers doing their jobs around. A large pool with lion shapes fountain situated in mansion after a few walk.

Nearly 2 minutes later Rudrajeet and Dasya reached to the office room, Rudrajeet showed his eyes to scanner and unlocked the door.

The office was adorned with rich furnishing, plush leather chairs, and a grand oak desk. The walls were filled with photographs capturing moments of happiness between Rudrajeet and Taniya.

A meticulously organized bookshelf stretched from floor to ceiling, filled with a vast collection of books.

Both men took their seats opposite each other, the large table serving as a formal divide between them. Rudrajeet began the conversation. "Dasya Kumar, aren't you the younger brother of Dasvi kumar?"

Dasya smiled. "Yes, I am" he replied with soft tone.

Rudrajeet's expression changed into nostalgia and sorrow. "Dasvi Kumar, he used to work with our group since our teenage years. He wasn't just a colleague; he was a great friend, someone I trusted like a brother."

Dasya listened attentively, his expression unchanged, giving Rudrajeet the space to share his memories.

"I really miss Dasvi," Rudrajeet confessed, his voice tinged with melancholy. "He sacrificed himself to protect Dhantara from Lionel. His sacrifice is the reason why Dhantara is now in my hands."

Dasya responded humbly. "Dasvi used to praise about you a lot, too. He admired your leadership and the way you managed everything."

"I saw you very rarely in those years," Rudrajeet mentioned, his memory reaching back to the past.

Dasya sighed, a hint of regret in his voice. "I had gone to London for some personal matters. But when I heard about the tragedy in Dhantara involving Lionel, I came back as soon as I could."

Dasya glanced at Golden lion statue and said "Lionel might be alive somewhere, but as long as you holds power in Dhantara, he won't come out of hiding. But many people fears him."

Rudrajeet nodded in agreement. "We've damaged him severely. He won't dare to come back, not with the losses we've inflicted upon him."

The conversation shifted, and Rudrajeet's tone grew more serious. "What about my sister, Taniya?" he inquired, his gaze piercing. "You might know the truth about what happened to her. Tell me."

Dasya revealed the truth, he told everything that happened including the threat his sister got from Mexican cartel and how he destroyed whole cartel to protect her.

Rudrajeet rose from his seat and embraced Dasya tightly, a genuine smile breaking across his face. "You're really a great person, just like Dasvi," Rudrajeet said with heartfelt appreciation. "Thanks a lot for this."

Dasya, still in Rudrajeet's embrace, gently pulled back and said, "Please, don't thank me. I have a request, though."

Rudrajeet, intrigued, looked at Dasya and asked, "What is it? You can ask anything."

Taking a deep breath, Dasya hesitated for a moment before confessing, "I have deep feelings for Taniya. I love her, and I want to marry her."

Rudrajeet's eyes widened in surprise, but he didn't interrupt. Dasya continued, "I understand this might be unexpected, but I promise to cherish her and protect her for the rest of my life. If she's willing, I want to make her happy."

After a thoughtful pause, Rudrajeet nodded "I trust you, Dasya. If Taniya is happy and willing to accept your proposal, then I have no objections. You have my blessing."

Rudrajeet and Dasya extended their hands, their fingers intertwining in a firm and decisive handshake. It was a silent agreement, a pact forged in trust and acceptance, sealing the bond between them.

The handshake was not just an agreement but also a promise - promise of loyalty, promise of supporting each other, promise of protecting Taniya.

Rudrajeet poured down wine on glass and offered it to Dasya, he accepted the wine.

Both cheered their glasses and together said "let's never break the bond, we'll end those whoever comes to destroy us. We'll fight together, we'll live together, we'll die together. For the family"

To be continued

Chapter 3 - For you

Flashback

The first light of dawn gently kissed the sky. Taniya knelt by the basin outside of their shelter. her hands submerged in the cool water and scrubbing the clothes against the smooth rocks.

Their home was a small shelter, barely more than a wooden room with a modest bed which they shared. In the backside of the shelter, there was a small toilet, hidden from views of others by wooden walls, cleaned meticulously every day by Rudrajeet, who took great care to ensure his sister's comfort and hygiene.

It was not ordinary morning, It was her birthday. While the world outside celebrate with joy and laughter on their birthday. Taniya's day began like any other, with struggles.

Rudrajeet, wiping sweat from his hair with a towel, entered the small room to find Taniya carefully hanging the freshly washed clothes on a rope for drying. He frowned. "Taniya, it's your birthday. Why are you still doing all this work? You should be resting, enjoying your day,"

Taniya looked at her brother, a soft smile on her lips despite the fatigue in her eyes. "Rudra, it's just another day. There's work to be done, and I don't mind. Birthdays are nice, but taking care of our everyday needs is important too."

Rudrajeet sighed. "I wish I could give you a proper celebration, Taniya. You deserve it."

She reached out and touched his hand. "Having you as my brother is the best gift I could ever ask for, Rudra. We might not have grand celebrations, but we have each other, and that's enough for me."

"I'm glad to hear that, Taniya." Rudrajeet's eyes softened and he offered a small smile.

She smiled back.

As he reached for his shirt, preparing to head out for work, Rudrajeet turned towards Taniya. "I'll be back soon. Take care while I'm gone."

Taniya nodded with reply "You too, Rudra. Please be careful out there."

With a final glance back at his sister, Rudrajeet stepped out of their shelter.

□

While walking towards his shop, Rudrajeet's sight caught attention of a poster. The image of a lion and the ominous message sent a shiver down his spine. It read - "WARNING! Serial killer with lion shaped tattoo preying on elite citizens including royals and stealing money from them. Be careful"

The news of this heinous crime didn't surprise Rudrajeet. He recalled the protest that had shaken the city to its core a few months ago, a protest against the royal family that had turned violent. More than hundred people lost their lives and nearly seventy people were injured.

Rudrajeet took off his glance from poster and continued his way to shop.

☐

After Rudrajeet reached his shop, he found the door locked from outside. Reality hit him hard – he had sold the shop for a mere 6000₹ in desperation for his sister who went ill and needed medical attention.

Thankfully, Taniya had survived, but now, Rudrajeet was facing struggles of finding a job in Dhantara.

Rudrajeet pulled out few coins from pocket and counted to confirm the amount — it was 12₹ which made Rudrajeet dissapointed.

"Aaj Taniya ka birthday celebrate karke rahunga mai" Rudrajeet vowed as he tightly clutched the coins.

Rudrajeet made his way to nearest bazaar where stalls were selling vegetables, teas, fishes. He had different plan in mind today, he wanted to do something daring for his sister.

Rudrajeet positioned himself on a nearby rock, blending into the surroundings as he observed the vibrant market.

His eyes scanning the hustle and bustle, seeking opportunities, studying them to seek opportunities.

After a while his gaze fell on a man in coal-black suit. Protected by three to four guards.

His presence and aura of elitness and wealth intrigued Rudrajeet. Rudrajeet watched from the shadows, his mind racing with how to execute his task.

Rudrajeet quickly came up with plan, walked away from the bustling main street, seeking out a quieter side street where he spotted a group of six beggar kids huddled together, their hungry eyes telling a tale of desperation.

"Are you hungry?" Rudrajeet kneeled down to match their heights.

The children, their stomachs rumbling, nodded eagerly. "Yes, we are," one of them replied, their voices soft yet hopeful.

Rudrajeet's eyes glinted with purpose. "There's a small shop nearby that charges 3₹ per plate of food," he said, gesturing towards the direction he had come from. "But I understand you don't have money." He paused, pulling out the few coins he had left, allowing them to glimmer in the faint light. "I have an offer for you. If you do a task for me, these coins will be yours, enough to get you all a warm meal."

Their eyes wide with curiosity. One of them, a young boy with dirt-smudged cheeks, spoke up. "What's the task?"

Rudrajeet motioned for them to move even closer, creating a circle. He glanced around cautiously, ensuring no prying ears were nearby, and then leaned in and revealed the task.

The children exchanged their glances for a minute then with an excitement they nodded.

□

"Do you have instant Korean noodles?" The man asked. He was standing in grocery shop, his fingers drummed on counter, waiting for shopkeeper to give what he needed.

The shopkeeper, recognizing the man as a regular customer, nodded respectfully. "Yes, Arjun sahab," he replied. "How many packets do you need?"

Arjun's lips curled into a satisfied smile. "I want 10 packets." He pulled out wallet, ready to pay for his purchase.

The shopkeeper nodded and turned around to retrieve the requested noodles from a nearby shelf.

Just as Arjun began to take out the money from his wallet, the beggar kids who were playing playfully nearby, rushed to Arjun's direction and collided with him, causing him to stumble backward and lose grip of his wallet.

The wallet slipped from his hand, falling on ground.

"Andhe hai kya lawde?" Arjun's frustration boiled over, he sternly yelled at the kids.

The beggar children, wide-eyed and apologetic, quickly muttered their apologies. "We're sorry, uncle."

Arjun's scowl deepened as he continued to scold them, his words laced with annoyance. "You shouldn't rush around in the market. Accidents can happen. Let people do their work in peace," he chastised.

The children, their faces etched with fear and guilt, huddled together. The youngest among them, a girl with big, sorrowful eyes, managed to stammer an apology. "We're sorry, sir."

Meanwhile, one step ahead. Rudrajeet approached from other side. Seizing the opportunity, using the diversion created by kids to snatch the wallet.

In a swift and silent move, he tossed the coins on the corner of ground for paying those children without Arjun noticing.

Rudrajeet skilfully grabbed the wallet and slipped it into his pocket when Arjun was busy on scolding them.

One of the daring beggar kid couldn't suppress a sly grin as he pointed at Rudrajeet's direction. "Hey mister, look over there!" he said, his laughter bubbling through his words. "Someone stole your wallet!"

Arjun's head whipped around just in time to catch a glimpse of Rudrajeet's retreating figure. His eyes narrowed in fury, and without a moment's hesitation, he barked out commands to his henchmen. "Catch that thief! Don't let him escape!"

His guards sprang into action, they raced after Rudrajeet, pushing away crowds.

Rudrajeet's speed was fast. He vaulted over crates of tomatoes, skillfully maneuvering through the market chaos. In a strategic move, he pushed the crates towards Arjun's guards, causing them to stumble and fall as they stepped on the squashed tomatoes.

Taking advantage of their momentary confusion, Rudrajeet dashed into a nearby alley, his footsteps echoing off the narrow walls.

The guards, undeterred, followed him.

Unfortunately the wallet fell down from his pocket but Rudrajeet continued running to dissappear from their views. The guards stopped near wallet and picked it up.

"Leave that bastard, let's give it back to boss" the guard said to other one. The other one wiped the sweat and declared. "Let me check if money is still there."

He opened the wallet, their eyes widened in surprise because the money was disappeared from wallet. They realized Rudrajeet fooled them to make them stop chasing him and he still have the money.

Rudrajeet took a moment to breath after losing them out of sight, he cautiously counted the cash he had taken from Arjun's wallet, and a wide smile broke across his face as he realized he had around 800₹ in his possession.

Rudrajeet decided to put his ill-gotten gains to good use. He headed to a nearby bakery shop.

He pulled the door open and entered. The bakery owner, a kindly man with a flour-dusted apron, approached him with a friendly smile. "What can I get for you, young man?" he asked.

Rudrajeet placed the order. "I'd like a small-sized chocolate cake, please, with 'Happy birthday Taniya' written on it."

The bakery owner's smile widened at the heartfelt request. "Of course, I'll get that for you. Please wait a moment," he said, disappearing into the bakery's kitchen to fulfill Rudrajeet's request.

After a brief wait, the owner emerged with a beautifully decorated chocolate cake, the words 'Happy birthday Taniya' elegantly written across its surface. Rudrajeet's eyes lit up with gratitude as he accepted the cake. "Thank you so much," he said, his voice sincere.

Curious about the cost, Rudrajeet inquired, "How much is it?"

The owner considered the moment of kindness and replied, "It's 200₹, young man."

Rudrajeet handed over the money. "Thank you," he said once more, his appreciation evident, before he carefully cradled the cake in his arms and walked away.

□

The day was transforming into evening, Dhantara's busy streets had grown silent and an eerie stillness settled over the city as night approached.

Rudrajeet fastened his pace on the quietening roads. His shelter was a distance away from his current location.

Rudrajeet slowed down the pace when his eyes fell on a teenage boy walking into dark alley. What caught his attention was the distinctive lion-shaped tattoo adorning the boy's neck. The same symbol that had been described in the warning poster he had seen earlier at road.

Rudrajeet decided to follow him into the alley. He entered the alley cautiously, maintaining the distance to not draw attention. His footsteps were hushed and his eyes locked on this boy ahead.

The twists and turns of the narrow path played tricks with the shadows, making it increasingly difficult to keep track of the boy. Despite Rudrajeet's best efforts, he eventually lost sight of him.

He didn't want to give up. Rudrajeet continued exploring the maze-like paths of the dark alley, his eyes darting from corner to corner in search of the mysterious teenager.

After several minutes of persistent searching, his ears suddenly caught a chilling sound that pierced the silence of the night – a loud, bone-chilling scream. The blood in his veins ran cold, and he instinctively followed the source of the scream.

When Rudrajeet reached to the source of scream, he saw three injured men lying on the ground, pain etched across their faces. One of them, struggling to catch his breath, spotted Rudrajeet and managed to speak between gasps of pain.

"A boy... attacked us," he wheezed, his voice strained. "He's after our boss now."

Rudrajeet's brows furrowed in concern. "Where did he go?"

The injured man pointed shakily to the right. "That way," he replied, his finger trembling as he indicated the direction.

Rudrajeet nodded. "Thank you" he replied and sprinted towards that indicated direction.

After a moment of running, Rudrajeet was stopped by a crying sound from a dark corner. He turned there and saw Arjun, the same man he had seen earlier in the market.

Arjun's face was etched in fear, his body trembling, and in front of him stood the teenage boy with knife.

"HEY! STOP IT WHOEVER THE FUCK YOU ARE." Rudrajeet's voice echoed, hoping to draw his attention.

The boy turned around, his eyes glowing an unsettling shade of red in the darkness. A sinister grin crept across his face, sending shivers down Rudrajeet's spine. The smile on the boy's face giving sense of true psychopath.

Rudrajeet swallowed hard, trying to steady his own nerves. He stood his ground, his eyes locked with the boy's, refusing to back down.

He was stepping forward Rudrajeet slowly, making Rudrajeet to prepare for danger.

Rudrajeet placed Taniya's cake aside.

The boy lunged at him with the knife, his eyes gleaming with malicious intent.

Rudrajeet dodged the boy's vicious slashes, his body moving with a dancer's grace, narrowly evading the blade. Seizing an opportune moment, he struck back, his fist connecting with the boy's face. The impact made the boy stagger, but he retaliated fiercely, delivering a powerful kick to

Rudrajeet's chest. The force sent Rudrajeet sprawling onto the ground, momentarily disoriented.

Undeterred, the boy advanced, attempting to stab Rudrajeet's face. With adrenaline-fueled strength, Rudrajeet grabbed the boy's wrist, his fingers clenching around the hilt of the knife, preventing it from reaching its deadly mark. Gritting his teeth, Rudrajeet fought back, kicking the boy squarely in the stomach, causing him to gasp for breath then he pushed the boy aside.

Rudrajeet rose to his feet, brushing off the dust from his clothes.

The boy stood up, his expression angry. He charged at Rudrajeet again.

Rudrajeet moved back towards the alley wall. Just as the boy lunged forward, Rudrajeet sidestepped with agile precision, causing the boy's knife to crash into the unforgiving brick wall, the sound of metal meeting stone ringing through the air.

Rudrajeet grabbed the boy's head, his grip firm and unyielding, and slammed it against the wall not once, but three times then he pushed away the boy.

The boy, determined not to be defeated, managed to stay on his feet, albeit unsteadily. He touched his forehead, feeling the warm trickle of blood, his eyes narrowing with a mix of pain and fury.

Before the boy could launch his next move, Rudrajeet's quick thinking came into play. He swiftly grabbed a stone from the ground, his fingers closing around it. With precision honed from desperation, he hurled the stone at the boy's face, causing the boy's grip on the knife to loosen involuntarily.

Rudrajeet lifted the knife. With a quick slash through the air, the blade found its mark, leaving a shallow cut on the boy's chest. The killer, seething with pain and rage, attempted to retaliate with a punch, but Rudrajeet, anticipating the attack, bent down, narrowly avoiding the blow.

Both turned around against each other, Rudrajeet aimed the knife at the boy's face and threw it. In a desperate attempt to defend himself, the killer raised his hand, inadvertently blocking the attack. The knife plunged into his arm, eliciting a cry of pain from him.

Rudrajeet swiftly jumping forward and pulling away the knife from arm. He slashed the knife and successfully cut the boy's finger, forcing a cry of agony from his lips

Clutching his bleeding hand, the boy accepted his defeat. In he glanced around and spotted an apartment wall with a pipeline. Without a second thought, he climbed up the pipeline and jumped to unknown person's balcony.

He leaped from the apartment's balcony to a nearby window ledge, using pipes and ledges as footholds.

Bounding effortlessly from one object to another, he reached the rooftop, his silhouette blending into the night. He landed on someone's terrace with a soft thud, his eyes scanning the surroundings one last time.

In the blink of an eye, he was gone.

The fight was finally over, a calm relief washed over Rudrajeet's face.

Breathing heavily, Rudrajeet turned to Arjun. "Are you alright? Are you safe now?"

Arjun nodded. "Yes, I'm safe. Thanks to you."

"Your men, they're injured, but they aren't bleeding. I think they need help." Rudrajeet revealed.

Arjun's eyes widened in realization. "I see. Thank you for your restraint."

As Arjun glanced at Rudrajeet's clothes, recognition flickered in his eyes. "Wait a minute, you're the boy who stole my wallet in the market, aren't you?"

He nodded with guilt. "Yes, I did. It's for my sister" he confessed with an apology. "I'm extremely sorry."

Rudrajeet pulled out the remaining money from his pocket. "I'm returning your money."

But Arjun waved his hand dismissively. "No need. Keep it. Consider it a gift for your sister's birthday."

Instead, he handed Rudrajeet a card. "Take this. Tomorrow, come to my office. Vihaan Kumar, the new head of the Royal family, is arranging jobs for people like you. There might be an opportunity for you."

Rudrajeet's eyes widened with gratitude. "Thank you so much! I can't express how grateful I am."

Arjun smiled warmly. "It's the least I can do. Take care of your sister. Good luck."

Rudrajeet nodded gratefully, his heart swelling with hope. He turned around, bidding Arjun goodbye, and ran back to his shelter.

□

Taniya's eyes lit up with joy when she unpacked the box which Rudrajeet carried to home.

Rudrajeet placed the cake on a table and hurriedly searched for candles. "Wait, I have something more," he said, his eyes sparkling with anticipation. He placed the candles on the cake.

Taniya eyed the cake, her curiosity piqued. "This cake looks expensive. Where did you get the money from, Rudra?"

Rudrajeet hesitated for a moment, then smiled and lied, "I saved up a little from odd jobs."

"I wanna share something" Taniya glanced at his words. "Tomorrow we're going to somewhere. It's for job under royal family leading by Vihaan, I need to do something Taniya. Today we're celebrating under this small shelter but soon we will celebrate under a mansion. I'll give you the royal life because our blood is royal blood"

Touched by his words, Taniya's eyes welled up with gratitude. "I love you, Rudra. Thank you for everything."

Rudrajeet embraced his sister, his arms wrapping around her protectively. Together, they held a plastic knife, symbolizing unity and love, and cut the cake together.

To be continued

Important (read this first)

When I started writing this book, many people added this in their reading list and still adding. But please atleast read if you genuinely added my book, I know some prefer reading completed book but it hurts knowing people only adding book in reading list but not actually reading them.

Also few people stopped reading because of not seeing romance. I want to tell you all that this book is story rooted, means I completely focus on storyline and character development before I show romance. So romance angle will take time, it's just 3-4 chapters and 2 prologue. You cannot explain instant romance.

I've planned a whole trilogy story and I need your support when I'm writing. There are many people who are reading on-going story like Mumbai to manhattan or Royal alliance

Then why don't you read this one? Is it because of not seeing romance quickly? I can't ruin my story to satisfy mass readers. Jo story jaisa hai waisa rahega bas.

Chapter 4 - The Royal celebration

---

4 years later after Dasya and Rudrajeet's meeting.

In the massive hall of Rudrajeet's mansion, vibrant hues of traditional Indian fabrics draped around the walls, casting a warm, inviting glow upon the grand celebration of Taniya's birthday.

Elegantly dressed mafia men and their wives, attire a fusion of traditional Indian silhouettes and modern embellishments, moved gracefully through the room.

Women wore expensive sarees in colour of gold, blue, red and emerald greens. Their sarees designated with embroidery sequins that glittered in soft light. Men were dressed in sherwani and some of were in their stylist coat suit.

The sounds of classical Indian music filled the mansion's hall, setting a melodious backdrop to the evening's festivities. Traditional instruments like sitars and tabla created a harmonious music.

The grand celebration came to a momentary halt as the guests' attention was drawn to the sight outside the mansion. A hushed whisper swept through the room like a gentle breeze, and all eyes turned towards the entrance where a large, sleek Mercedes had pulled up.

Rudrajeet stepped out of the Mercedes, his presence commanding attention. He was dressed impeccably in a red suit, accentuated by a crisp white shirt and stylish blue jeans.

The mafia guests inside the mansion bowed down together to show their respect of Rudrajeet's presence. The room fell silent, the only sound being the soft rustle of fabrics as the guests lowered their heads in deference.

Rudrajeet, flanked by his loyal bodyguards, walked with purpose and confidence towards the entrance of the mansion.

When Rudrajeet entered inside, a wave of smile spread among mafias, their eyes lightning up.

One of the guests approached him, questioned him after a small handshake. "Mr Ray, where's your sister? we cannot see her around even though tonight is her birthday."

Rudrajeet glanced at his right-hand man, Abhineet. who was nearbyHe signaled Abhineet to join him. Abhineet quickly finished his drink and made his way over to Rudrajeet.

Rudrajeet teased him playfully, a smirk playing on his lips. "Abhineet, you started drinking without me?"

Abhineet, realizing his mistake, quickly apologized. "I'm sorry, boss. It won't happen again."

Rudrajeet chuckled. "Arre Mai mazak kar raha tha. Taniya kaha hai? tera zimmedari tha na usko yaha laane ka jabtak Mai na aau."

Abhineet shook his head slightly. "She won't come out without her brother by her side."

Rudrajeet flickered his forehead. "Party handle kar sakta hai lekin jiske liye party rakha usko nahi."

Abhineet rolled his head. "Usne boli ki jabtak mera bhai nahi aayega tabtak nahi aaunga mai, 20 minute se samjhaya. Aayi nahi woh."

Rudrajeet's smiled widened with happiness. He excused himself from the conversation and gracefully made his way upstairs.

◻

Taniya sat by the old photographs, each frame showing the memories from teen life to adult life, from living at slum area to living at royal mansion, from nobody to respected family of Dhantara.

A soft knock grabbed her attention. Taniya's heart skipped a beat with excitement. Rising from chair, she ran to pull the door, revealing Rudrajeet standing with warm smile on lips and his hands holding a bouquet of roses.

"Happy birthday cutie." Rudrajeet stretched his hand to pass the bouquet.

Taniya embraced her brother in a tight hug, her arms wrapping around him. She pulled back slowly and looked into his eyes. "Where were you? I was waiting for you Rudra."

Rudrajeet understood her feelings, he gently cupped her face. "I didn't forget, Taniya. That's why I came back from work as quickly as I could."

"Now, let's go to the hall together. Our guests are waiting to celebrate this special day with us," he said, leading the way with a loving smile. Hand in hand both walked towards the hall, ready to share their joy.

◻

The crowd erupted into cheers when they saw Rudrajeet and Taniya appeared at top of staircase. The stairs glowed with golden light when Taniya stepped her feet on it.

Abhineet, recognizing the perfect moment to address the gathering, stepped forward and took hold of the microphone. "Ladies and gentlemen," Abhineet's voice boomed, capturing the room's attention. "Let's welcome the king of Dhantara, Rudrajeet Ray. Who is not only king of Dhantara but respected godfather of underworld system. By his side, stands Taniya whose birthday we're celebrating with royalty."

The room filled with applause and cheers once more, the guests raising their glasses in a toast to honor Rudrajeet and Taniya.

Mafia members approached Taniya. One of the mafia women, dressed elegantly in a traditional saree, greeted Taniya with a warm smile. "Taniya, you look absolutely stunning tonight. Happy birthday! Your presence adds grace to this celebration."

Taniya, humbled by the compliment, replied with gratitude. "Thank you so much. I'm truly honored to be here, surrounded by such wonderful people."

Rudrajeet noticed a man with blonde hair and blue eyes, wearing black suit. Observing him from a distance. Sensing an unspoken connection, Rudrajeet turned to Taniya and gently touched her arm. "Wait here, Taniya. I'll be back in a moment."

Rudrajeet made his way towards his office, the man followed him behind closely.

□

"James, it's great to have you in our party," Rudrajeet said, extending a welcoming hand towards the mysterious man.

"I shall thank you for inviting me. Dhantara looks more developed and better than our city Harran," James replied, his gaze fixed on the cityscape outside the window.

Rudrajeet nodded thoughtfully, acknowledging James' observation. "Indeed, Dhantara has seen remarkable growth in recent years. We've worked hard to make it a city of opportunities and progress."

"Rudrajeet, you see," James began, his voice carrying a tinge of bitterness, "my father worked tirelessly to make Harran more messed up than before. It's a city drowning in chaos."

Rudrajeet looked at James. "Perhaps it's time someone stepped forward to change the course of Harran's fate. A new leader, someone with vision and dedication, could transform the city into a beacon of hope and progress."

James met Rudrajeet's gaze. "I wish I could," he replied earnestly. "But right now, my focus is elsewhere. I'm busy with my family and helping my bestfriend who is desperate to save his family."

Rudrajeet's eyes met James', a silent understanding passing between them. He reached into his pocket and pulled out a folded piece of paper, carefully unfolding it and placing it on the desk. "James, I have a proposition for you."

James glanced down at the paper, his brow furrowing in curiosity. The paper was about details of gun smuggling operation.

"We're looking at a transaction worth 800 crores. These guns are crucial for our operations, and I need someone I can trust to ensure their safe passage," Rudrajeet explained, his gaze steady. "I believe you have the skills and determination to help us."

James took a deep breath. He picked up the pen on the desk and signed the paper, committing himself to the operation.

"I'll help you, Rudrajeet, but I need some time," James said, his voice steady. "Right now, my focus is on completing my goal."

Rudrajeet nodded. "I understand, James. Focus on whatever you have in mind, we'll proceed later as we planned."

□

Reyansh, the CEO of a company in Rajasthan, watched Taniya from across the room as she engaged in conversation with female guests. A sly grin crept onto his face. "Taniya looks hot."

His friend raising an eyebrow, responded. "But you have a wife already, don't forget Kainaat."

Reyansh shrugged, attempting to downplay his comment. "It's just a compliment, nothing more than that."

His collegue unimpressed, shot back, "Doesn't look like a compliment, but a comment you've passed on her. Remember, words have weight, especially when they come from someone in your position."

"Hello, Mr. Reyansh," a voice interrupted Reyansh's thoughts, and he felt a hand on his shoulder. Startled, he turned around and saw Rudrajeet standing there.

Reyansh's heart skipped a beat, hoping that Rudrajeet hadn't overheard his earlier conversation.

Rudrajeet's eyes flickered, he asked. "How's the drink?"

For a moment, Reyansh hesitated, his composure slightly shaken. "It's... it's good," he stammered, trying to regain his poise.

Reyansh again tried to attempt to steer the conversation away from the previous awkward moment, glanced around the opulent interior of the mansion. "Your mansion looks so beautiful," he remarked, trying to strike up a casual conversation. "How much does it cost?"

Rudrajeet, his smile enigmatic. "Actually, it's none of your business," he replied smoothly. "But let me tell you, it isn't cheap. The mansion is more expensive than anyone presented in this hallway."

Reyansh, taken aback by Rudrajeet's response, nodded awkwardly.

□

As the night wore on, the atmosphere in the mansion buzzed with laughter, clinking glasses, and the delightful aroma of delicious foods.

The dining room became hub of lively discussion between mafias, they were served by waiters from famous restaurants.

Hours later, the dining concluded, and the guests, now content and satisfied, bid their hosts farewell.

When the clock struck midnight, the guests departed the mansion one by one, their cars elegantly lined up outside.

Inside of mansion, Rudrajeet scanned around workers engaged at cleaning in a post-party cleanup. A satisfaction washes over him, he was happy that he celebrated her birthday in grand level without any regret. Yet, his attention was drawn elsewhere. Taniya, his beloved sister, was nowhere to be found.

He searched around for her but all he got was 'we didn't see her'.

His intuition guided him to the terrace, a place where Taniya often sought solace. He stepped into the elevator, its doors smoothly closing behind him. Moments later, he ascended to the terrace. The night breeze greeted him as he stepped into the open space, and there she was, his sister, gazing up at the stars.

Rudrajeet walked towards Taniya. "Are you happy, Taniya? I kept my promise."

Taniya offered a smile. "Yes, I'm happy."

Rudrajeet, sensing there might be more to her emotions, persisted gently, "Is something bothering you, Taniya? You can tell me."

Taniya hesitated for a moment before confessing. "I miss Dasya," she admitted.

Rudrajeet was surprised by her confession. "But why...?"

Taniya looked at her brother. "Because he was my husband."

Rudrajeet furrowed his eyes in frustration. "But Taniya, he doesn't deserved to be missed. Especially what he did when you were pregnant."

Taniya remained silent.

He turned around to retreat from conversation. "Brother, wait" Rudrajeet stopped in his track after her call.

He glanced at her eyes which was close to drop tears. She confessed "I miss him sometimes and today I missed him because I saw all these mafias with their wives. I miss having that companionship. I know he did wrong with me last year but for 3 years he treated me like queen...I'm sorry Rudra."

Rudrajeet moved close to an architect with flowers, he pressed his hands against the architect. "I understand but Taniya...I feel like killing Dasya, it's about to be 2 years now I'm controlling myself just because he's your husband. If someone looks at my sister with bad intention then I never show mercy but DASYA IS..."

He stopped in the middle of his speech, kissing his sister on forehead. "Just remember, in this world your brother loves you more than anyone."

She felt relaxed from hearing this from her brother. Taniya put her head on his chest, hugging him softly. Rudrajeet held her tightly.

□

"What did I do? what the fuck are you doing with me?" Reyansh was knelt down, tears streaming from his eyes.

"FUCKING EXPLAIN TO ME!!' He pleaded again, searching any signs of explanation from Abhineet who was standing infront of him, holding a bottle of dangerous acid.

"Mr Reyansh rathore" Abhineet called out his name in dark monstrous tone. "King of Rajasthan, a fucking CEO."

He walked to blood stained Reyansh surrounded by Rudrajeet's men. "You insulted Rudrajeet's sister. You've passed vile comments on her and for that you are here."

Reyansh's face was contorted with fear and regret. "I didn't mean it that way! It was a joke. I'll apologize to her, to Rudrajeet, please leave me alone."

"Words have consequences when it comes to godfather of Dhantara, even a small words against his sister have big consequences." Abhineet stated.

"She's not only his sister, she's my sister too. Rudrajeet never takes these matters lightly so he ordered me to take care of it."

Reyansh's whole body began trembling in fear when Abhineet closed the pacing with his steps. "ABHINEET! Please consider my apology. I'm sorry, I will never do something like that."

"LISTEN YOU IDIOT" Abhineet thundered, grabbing Reyansh's have tightly and making him eye contact with his. "Rudrajeet burned down the whole fucking forest for his sister. He will do anything for her including burning the eyes which insulted Taniya's honor."

"Abhineet don't do this, d-"

He poured down the whole acid on Reyansh's face. The dark room echoed with Reyansh's agonized screams, the acidic substance searing his skin with an excruciating, relentless pain. Within moments, his face began to melt, the skin bubbling and dissolving into grotesque streams of flesh, revealing the raw bones beneath.

□

"The moon looks so beautiful from Dhantara," the lady said, her voice smooth as silk, as she sipped her red wine in the back of the luxurious black car. She was dressed in a short vintage outfit, a daring choice that revealed her tempting décolletage, the fabric a brackish shade that accentuated her elegance. The ensemble featured elegant dolman sleeves, perfectly complemented by her stylish platform heels.

Beside her, a man glanced at her with a smirk. "Doesn't it look beautiful from Dhantara always?"

"Oh Rehaan, it doesn't," she replied, a smile playing on her lips. "The nightsky always looks so chaotic from Dhantara. But tonight is different because godfather of Dhantara is happy after years of intense violence he had committed."

"Did you enjoy the royal party?" Rehaan questioned curiously.

"I did" she replied softly. "It reminded me of my dad. He used to organize small events for me often in grand way."

Rehaan smiled in agreement. "Rudrajeet has a way of making everything grand for his sister."

Her gaze turned distant for a moment. "Tonight, he didn't talk to me."

Rehaan, ever the optimist, suggested, "You know, you could always approach him, make a move. He's not the type to shy away from a good conversation."

A playful glint entered her eyes. "One day, Rehaan, I'll make this Mr criminal come to me." She declared.

Rehaan impressed by her confidence, poured down another round of wine into her glass and raised his own glass in a toast. "I'll wait for that day, Navisha."

To be continued

Chapter 5 - I love you for thousand times

Rudrajeet groggily woke up, his head throbbing from the effects of alcohol. He found himself sprawled on the red sofa in the living room.

He pushed himself up from the red sofa, trying to regain his composure.

"Goodmorning sir" Rudrajeet's attention was caught by kitchen staff who was passing by. He offered him a glass of water.

Rudrajeet accepted the water and too a sip, still groggy, rubbed his temples and met the staff's gaze. "What happened last night after the party? I don't remember much."

Staff member responded softly. "You came out from the terrace, sir, and you had quite a bit to drink. Sir Abhineet tried to escort you to your bedroom, but you insisted on spending here in the living room."

Rudrajeet ran a hand through his disheveled hair, trying to recall the details. Fragments of the conversation with his sister surfaced in his memory, making him wince with regret. "What about Taniya? I acted rude towards her last night. Is she alright?"

The staff member reassured him, "She's sleeping in her room, sir. You don't have to worry."

Rudrajeet sighed with relief.

Rudrajeet's henchman rushed into the living room, a look of urgency on his face. He quickly called out to Rudrajeet. "BOSS!"

Rudrajeet placed the glass on table and asked. "What happened!?"

The henchman mentioned Taniya's name, causing Rudrajeet's heart to skip a beat. "What happened to Taniya?" he demanded, his voice rising with worry.

The henchman didn't waste any time. "You need to come with me," he said urgently, motioning for Rudrajeet to follow.

Without another word, Rudrajeet followed his henchman, his heart pounding in his chest with fear of worst scenarios.

As he entered the room, he witnessed Taniya's face expressed with pain, screaming in agony and pain. Abhineet and the guards were trying their best to calm her down and provide support.

Abhineet noticed Rudrajeet stepping inside of room, he quickly walked to him.

"Rudra, it's time for her delivery." Abhineet informed. "She needs to be in hospital immediately before something bad ha-"

He was cut off by Rudrajeet who rushed to her side. Rudrajeet gently cupped Taniya's tear-streaked cheeks, his voice tender yet firm. "Taniya, sister, don't cry. We're taking you to the hospital. Everything will be fine, I promise."

She nodded weakly. "Please do something Rudra."

"GET THE CARS READY." Rudrajeet barked orders, his voice echoing through the room.

He gestured firmly at Abhineet, indicating the need for his assistance. Without a moment's hesitation, Abhineet nodded in understanding, joining Rudrajeet to carefully lift Taniya, cradling her in their arms. Together, they hurried towards the garage.

□

Her hands clutched at the seat, fingers digging into the fabric, seeking something to hold onto amid the intense waves of pain. Taniya's jaw clenched, teeth biting down on her lower lip, as if trying to endure the pain in silence.

Rudrajeet couldn't see her pain anymore, his face was watered by tears. This was the first time he saw her in pain and it was unwatchable for him.

Gently, he reached out for her hand. He began speaking soothing words.

"Sister, I'm right here with you," he whispered, his tone soft and reassuring. "You're not alone, and we're on our way to the hospital. The doctors will take good care of you, and soon, we'll be welcoming your little one into the world."

"Dekhna Mai unka accha mama banunga, bohot jagah ghumane lejaunga. Gifts dunga bohot saare, tu bas thora sa dard sehle."

She found solace on his words, softly putting her head on his shoulder.

Rudrajeet caressed her hair tenderly and sang her favorite song to make her feel better. "I have died everyday waiting for you. Darling, don't be afraid. I have loved for. For a thousand years."

He stopped in between, his voice cracking in sadness.

A smile wrapped on Taniya's lips, she pressed Rudrajeet's palm tightly and finished the line with her melancholic voice. "I love you for thousand times..."

Eventually their cars stopped outside of Hospital. Not wasting any seconds, Rudrajeet opened the gate, coming out from car with his sister.

He lifted her up with both hands, his steps closing to hospital's entrance in fast pace.

But before he could enter, his eyes scanned the area, noticing the fear in the public's eyes due to the sight of armed guards. He turned to his men, his tone stern and authoritative.

"Don't bring guns to the hospital, are you all mad?" Rudrajeet's words cut through the tension. "My sister's life depends on this hospital. Show some respect."

His men, understanding the gravity of situation. Bowed down in obeying his order. One by one, they placed their guns on car trunk.

Abhineet pulled the entrance door, helping Rudrajeet to go inside.

Nurses and doctors hurried to Rudrajeet when they recognized him. Their faces were filled with surpriseness.

One of them, a silk haired nurse asked. "Sir, what's the emergency?"

Rudrajeet explained them about her delivery. The medical team sprang into action. One nurse swiftly fetched a stretcher, carefully placing Taniya upon it. With practiced efficiency, they maneuvered the stretcher towards the delivery room.

Rudrajeet following closely behind, his eyes never leaving his sister. But in matter of seconds, they entered into delivery room.

A doctor blocked Rudrajeet's path. "Sir, you cannot enter the room, I'm sorry. I request you to wait there for report."

Rudrajeet held onto the doctor's hand, his voice cracking with emotion as he pleaded, "Please, save her. She's everything to me."

The doctor, taken aback by the sight of the powerful King of Dhantara reduced to tears, gently placed a reassuring hand on Rudrajeet's arm. "I will do everything in my power to save her. Trust me."

With a deep breath, he nodded. "Thank you doc."

Rudrajeet found a glimmer of hope, putting his faith on medical professionals.

The doctor disappeared from his sight after a calm smile. Leaving him alone at waiting room.

□

Abhineet, seeing Rudrajeet's anxiety, placed a reassuring hand on his shoulder. "Stay calm, she will be fine."

Rudrajeet nodded, appreciating Abhineet's attempt to console him. After a moment of silence, Rudrajeet's eyes glinted with determination. "I need to welcome the child with something special," he stated.

"A gift?" Abhineet raises his eyebrows.

"Yes," Rudrajeet affirmed. "And I want you to help me choose. You've worked in an orphanage before; you know what would be meaningful."

Abhineet, always ready to support Rudrajeet, readily agreed. "Of course, I'd be honored to help."

The two friends walked out of the hospital to visit nearest mall.

□

Abhineet and Rudrajeet entered the toyshop, the air was filled with the scent of new plastic and the soft hum of children's laughter. Rows of colorful toys adorned the shelves, capturing the essence of innocence and joy. Rudrajeet's eyes scanned the displays.

Rudrajeet's eyes twinkled with mischief as he reached for a bright, neon-colored Nerf gun from the shelf. He examined it with interest before turning to Abhineet, a playful grin on his face.

"What do you think about this? It looks quite attractive, doesn't it?" Rudrajeet asked, his tone light.

Abhineet crossed his arms. "A nerf gun? are you planning to train the baby for future battle?" He teased.

Rudrajeet chuckled, realizing the impracticality of his choice. "I suppose it might be a bit too advanced for a newborn," he admitted, placing the Nerf gun back on the shelf. "Let's find something more suitable and age-appropriate."

They continued their search for new toys, both separated to different sides and started looking.

Rudrajeet was still confused what to choose, he was fascinated by Lego sets but he was aware that it won't be suitable for babies and it might cause danger if the baby swallow a piece.

"Hey" Rudrajeet turned around Abhineet's side.

Abhineet carefully cradled the soft, pink bunny toy in his hands and approached Rudrajeet with a warm smile. "How about this one, sir? It's soft, cuddly, and perfect for a newborn. Plus, it's adorable," Abhineet suggested, holding the bunny up for Rudrajeet to see.

Rudrajeet's eyes softened as he gazed at the fluffy toy. He nodded appreciatively. "You're right, Abhineet. It's perfect. Let's go with this one."

Rudrajeet took the soft toy from Abhineet's hand, walking to cashier for payment.

Before he could reach there, he noticed a kid crying near bookshelf and his mother scolding at him.

Rudrajeet approached the mother and her child with a warm smile. "Is everything alright?"

The mother, clearly surprised and respectful, recognized Rudrajeet and replied.

"Oh, sir I didn't expect you to be here. I'm really blessed to see King of Dhantara in here and yes everything is fine. It's just that my son here really wants this comic book, even though I've already bought him a video game for birthday."

Rudrajeet's heart went out to the child's desire for the comic book. He asked "what's the little one's name?"

The mother answered."His name is Aarav Mehta, and I'm Mrs. Nehal Mehta."

Rudrajeet nodded and then knelt down to Aarav's eye level, addressing the child. "Happy birthday pal. Well, Aarav, it seems you really like that comic book, huh?"

Aarav's eyes lit up, and he nodded enthusiastically. "Yes, sir! I want it so much!"

Rudrajeet chuckled and then turned to Mrs. Mehta. "I can't help but understand Aarav's love for comics. It's a fantastic world in there. Would it be alright with you if I get it for him?"

Mrs. Mehta hesitated for a moment. "Sir, I appreciate the gesture, but I can't accept such a gift."

Rudrajeet reached into his wallet and pulled out 10,000₹. He offered it to Mrs. Mehta, saying, "Please, consider it a gift from me. I know how a simple comic book can bring joy to a child's heart. It would make me happy to see Aarav smile. And today is his birthday so take him to theater or restaurant, spend the day with him."

Mrs. Mehta was moved by Rudrajeet's kind gesture, and she finally accepted the money with gratitude. Aarav's face lit up as he clutched the coveted comic book in his hands, his mother's acceptance, and Rudrajeet's generosity filling their hearts with warmth and appreciation.

She thanked him once more, walking out of toyshop. Rudrajeet smiled, knowing that he will remember this wholesome moment forever.

Abhineet leaning back to wall, his arm crossed near chest. "You have a heart of gold, boss. Not everyone would do what you just did back there."

"Thank you, Abhineet. But it's the little things that matter the most, don't you think? Let's go welcome the newest member of our family now."

A phone vibrated from Rudrajeet's pocket, he snatched it out from there and saw his henchman calling him. Picking up quickly, he questioned. "Hey! Any report about Taniya?"

Abhineet moved closer with excitement, awaiting for news. But what happened next left him stunned.

Rudrajeet's phone collapsed on ground, he kneeled down, tears streaming from his eyes.

□

"Due to heavy blood loss, we couldn't save her and her baby. It was too late, I'm terribly sorry." Doctor said, lowering his eyes from Rudrajeet's gaze.

Rudrajeet's eyes were red in anger and tears. "What's your name...doctor?" Rudrajeet asked darkly. His voice was threatening and scary.

"As...Ashok mehta" his voice shaking in fear.

Rudrajeet grabbed Ashok's white collar tightly, slamming him against the wall. "ASHOK FUCKING MEHTA! WHAT THE FUCK YOU TOLD ME? YOU WILL SAVE HER! RIGHT?"

Doctor Ashok gasped for air, his back pressed against the cold wall. "I...I did everything I could. The loss was just too much. I'm sorry, I really am."

Rudrajeet's rage was palpable, but he released the doctor. His voice trembled with anger and pain as he spoke. "Sorry won't bring her back, she was my only family."

Doctor Mehta could only nod, his eyes filled with regret.

Rudrajeet turned to Taniya's dead body. Her closed eyes and pale body broke his heart into million pieces, he kneeled down near her body. Trembling hands reached out to clasp Taniya's lifeless ones. Tears blurred his vision as he spoke, his voice breaking with desperation.

"Taniya, please... Please come back. I can't do this without you. You're my strength, my everything. Life will be a living hell without you. Who will take care of me like you did? Who will I live for?"

"Mujhe chodh ke mat ja...aaj mai mama banne wala tha, tere bacche ko dekhna chahta tha, apne haatho se khilana chahta tha. Kitna kuch socha tha, ek aur celebration karunga socha tha. Mat ja Taniya..." He pressed his lips against her cold hand, his silent sobs filling the room, a heartbreaking melody of grief and loss. But there was no response, only a profound silence, echoing the void in his heart.

Rudrajeet slapped Ashok tightly, making him fall back but before he could fall. Rudrajeet's hand gripped his tie and he released his pent-up fury on him by punches.

One punch on jaw, second punch on cheeks, third punch on left side of face. Even nurses weren't able to stop him and they were scared to call the security because of Rudrajeet's henchmen.

Blood splattered across the floor, he sought a fleeting release from the overwhelming pain, but it only intensified the void left by his sister's absence.

After several relentless punches, Rudrajeet finally pushed Ashok away, sending him crashing into a nearby chair. The doctor slumped, dazed and bruised.

"YOU TOOK EVERYTHING AWAY FROM ME." Rudrajeet spat at him, the saliva landed on Ashok's eyes. He walked away with heavy steps, wiping tears from eyes with arms but tears were unstoppable.

Ashok regained his composure, he wiped away the saliva from his bruised lips.

That silk haired nurse helped him to rise from chair. "It's going to be alright, you did everything you could."

Ashoke with shaky body, approached to window. Holding onto the window's edge for support, Ashok cried out.

"I failed... for the first time in my career. The King of Dhantara trusted me, and I... I disappointed him."

Other nurse replied to his remorse softly. "You're a brilliant doctor, Ashok. Sometimes, despite our best efforts, we face situations beyond our control. It's not your fault."

"But I promised him... I promised Don Rudrajeet that I would save her. I failed to keep that promise. How will I face him now?" Ashok's voice broke.

He sadly looked at Taniya's body "Since years, many royal families treated us like ants but Rudrajeet never treated us like them. He requested me like he's a normal brother, fearing for his sister. He cried infront of me. HE HAD HOPE WHEN I TOLD HIM THAT I'LL SAVE HER."

Both nurses fell silent. Ashok sniffled, wiping his tears. "I can't bear the weight of this failure, I can't bear the dissapointment in his eyes. I deserved that harsh beating."

One of the nurse moved close to him, "We'll be here for you. The king may be grieving now, but he will understand in time. Remember, you're human too. You did everything in your power. That's all anyone can ask for."

Ashok nodded. "Thank you both, I hope one day he forgives us."

Ashok's phone rang, he quickly picked it up when he saw it was his wife calling him. He answered the call. "Hey...honey."

"Hey, Ashok! Are you coming home soon? We need to get ready for Aarav's birthday celebration at the theater," his wife's voice echoed with excitement and anticipation.

Ashok managed to muster a weak smile. "Yes, I'll be there shortly. Just finishing up some work."

There was a pause on the other end of the line, then his wife's concerned voice filled the airwaves. "Is everything okay? Your voice sounds different."

His grip tightened on the phone as he struggled to find the right words. "I'll explain everything when I get home. Just need a little time," he said, his voice barely audible, choked with emotions.

"Alright, take your time. Whatever it is, please be safe, Aarav is waiting for you." She said with worry evident on her face.

Thankful for her understanding, Ashok whispered, "Thank you, dear. I love you." He kissed on the screen.

"I love you too, Ashok. See you soon." She said, kissing back before hanging up.

Ashok hung up the phone. He took a deep breath, trying to gather his strength before heading home to his family.

Suddenly, a thunderous noise reverberated through the room. The door swung open violently, propelled by a forceful kick. Ashok's eyes widened in terror as he saw Rudrajeet again. Standing infront of him.

Anger seemed increasing in his eyes. Sweat dripped down his temples, mingling with tears that traced salty paths down his cheeks.

Ashok's throat tightened, and he involuntarily gulped in fear.

"Sir, please forgive me. I can understand how you fe-" Ashok's voice faltered. Rudrajeet drew his pistol from back, aiming it at Ashok's forehead. He pulled the trigger.

Ashok's head jerked backward, a grotesque explosion of blood splattering gruesomely and painting the white walls.

The nurses who were standing nearby, screamed in pure fear when they saw their beloved doctor crumpled to the floor. His lifeless eyes staring into nothingness.

To be continued

Chapter 6 - Consequences

T he courtroom echoed with the decisive words of the judge, "The court grants bail to Mr. Rudrajeet upon posting a bail amount of 10 million rupees." Rudrajeet's lawyer nodded in acknowledgment.

Exiting courtroom, Rudrajeet was flanked by Abhineet and other guards. The sea of citizens gathered infront of courthouse, holding banners where harsh words were written against him.

"Murderer!" shouted one protester, the word cutting through the air like a serrated blade. Another banner declared, "Justice for the innocent doctor."

"YOUR BLOODY MONEY CANT BUY INNOCENCE"

"WE TRUSTED YOU ALOT"

"FUCK THESE ROYAL PEOPLE"

"LET'S BREAK CAPITALISM"

Roar of their words were getting louder, all of them were in mood of killing Rudrajeet badly right there. To stop them, police force formed a barricade and shields.

"You killed my husband! you stole the love of my life!" Rudrajeet stopped in his track after hearing this sentence.

He turned to his left, and there she was-the woman from the toy shop, her eyes ablaze with anger and grief. Beside her, Aarav, the child he had gifted a comic book, sobbed uncontrollably.

"I..I'm sorry" Rudrajeet muttered. Tears slowly dropping from his eyes, he couldn't believe that he destroyed the family who had smile on their faces for him.

She pulled out a bundle of cash around 15000₹ and roughly tossed it at Rudrajeet.

The cash fluttered in the air, landing at Rudrajeet's feet.

"You think you can buy everything, don't you?" she spat, her voice trembling with a blend of sorrow and rage. "You may have the power to control this city and manipulate the law, but you can't purchase someone's heart, especially one that you've shattered."

Rudrajeet stood frozen, the weight of the woman's words echoing in his mind. His voice wavered as he whispered to himself, "What have I become?"

Just as he was on the verge of an emotional breakdown, Abhineet intervened, grabbing Rudrajeet's hand with a firm grip. "Let's go, sir," Abhineet said, leading him toward the waiting car.

Numbly, Rudrajeet sank into the back seat. Abhineet took the front seat and directed the driver to start the car. The engine roared to life, drowning out the cacophony of the protesting crowd.

Inside of car, Rudrajeet remained lost in thoughts. He grabbed his forehead and began crying, tears flooding from his eyes to cheeks.

Abhineet tried to console Rudrajeet, saying, "Sir, don't let it get to you. We'll figure a way out of this mess."

Ignoring Abhineet's attempt to console him, Rudrajeet continued to cry. His voice as he said through tears.

"I lost everything, Abhineet. My sister, her child and now respect of these people."

□

Rudrajeet was sitting on warm sofa, his gaze fixed on TV screen which played old videos of happy days with his sister. In one of that video she was on Rollercoaster ride and Rudrajeet hugging her to not make her feel scared in there.

Rudrajeet sighed with grief. "My sister was scared...not because of that ride, but because of separating from me."

Abhineet standing nearby, observed his boss. "She'll always be part of our memories. I'm also feeling the same pain which you're feeling." He said with tearful eyes.

Rudrajeet didn't say anything, just acknowledged Abhineet's words with a nod.

Suddenly Abhineet's phone interrupted them with a call.

Seizing the device from his pocket, he answered the call. Initially indifferent, Rudrajeet's curiosity was piqued as he noticed Abhineet's face turned pale.

"Ok...I'll arrange everything." Abhineet hung up the call with a tense voice.

"Abhineet, what's going on?" Rudrajeet questioned, eyes fixed on him.

Abhineet, his forehead glistening with a sheen of sweat, hesitated before responding, "Sir, it's not a regular day. The six influential members of our group - Fratello, Rachael, Arman, Levi, Devraj, and Anirudh - are convening for a crucial meeting. They're uniting for something important. "

□

The meeting room felt heavily important, the walls had blend of light brown and dark hues that added a touch of class to the environment. A luxurious chandelier hung elegantly from the center of the ceiling, casting a warm glow across the room.

A large table, stationed directly beneath the chandelier, dominated the room. Encircled by dark leather chairs, each seat meticulously prepared with elegantly designed glasses by maid.

Soon those mafias occupied their places, leaving the central chair at the head of table for Rudrajeet.

male staff members entered the room, bearing a bottle of fine alcohol. They expertly poured the golden liquid into the waiting glasses, setting the stage for a meeting.

Rudrajeet entered the room with a mask of carefully crafted smile.

The atmosphere shifted as he took his place among the assembled mafia members, each eye keenly observing the man who usually wore a different demeanor.

Taniya's demise had left an indelible mark on Rudrajeet, transforming his usual aura into one colored by grief.

"So..." Rudrajeet sighed with a tired voice. "What is the reason for all of your gatherings today?"

Among them, Fratello, an old senior mafia was the first one to speak. "We're very sorry for what happened to your sister, it was very unfortunate. She was very br-"

"Sorry won't undo things" Rudrajeet snapped, cutting Fratello's words. His voice expressing the pain which he was hiding with fake smile.

Rudrajeet glared deadly at Fratello this time. "And I don't need condolences when it's coming from an old man who abandoned his sister after she lost her parents," he silenced Fratello by revealing the past which embarrassed him.

Another member, Levi spoke up, his voice smooth buy edged with caution.

"We got the news that you killed an innocent doctor infront of public... we're working together since 6 years and we did everything according to rules, just to keep us together."

Rudrajeet's jaw clenched, his hand forming fists on table. "It was just a mistake, I wasn't on right mind!"

Rachael, taking a deep breath. Gathered courage to address Rudrajeet, leaned forward. "Rudrajeet, do you realize your mistake has put all of us in danger? Killing an innocent man, especially a renowned doctor, has put our entire group at risk. Even after your bail, police will investigate on you further and this will lead them to expose us as well."

Understanding Rachael's concern. Rudrajeet replied. "I understand the gravity of our situation. Rest assured, I will find a solution to navigate through this storm. We cannot allow our empire to crumble under external pressure."

"We don't need a solution." A sudden voice interrupted them. The words were from the person with black jacket sitting at the opposite side of table, face to face with Rudrajeet.

He had long dark hair, reaching upto neck. That dark hair was hiding the scar which formed on his neck.

The person raised the glass of beer and took a sip from it. "We don't need a solution...we already have one."

All eyes shifted towards him, waiting for him to reveal his proposition. Rudrajeet, intrigued, turned his attention fully to the man with the scars. "Solution? what's that solution, Devraj?"

Devraj with a calm tone, unfolded the shocking plan. "We never wanted to say this but...we want to cut all ties with you, yahi ek raasta hai hamare paas."

Rudrajeet's eyes widened in shock, his voice betrayed a hint of disbelief. "Don't do jokes, Devraj. You can't be serious."

But Devraj's eyes remained resolute. "Everyone at this table agrees with me, Rudrajeet. We thought alot about it."

Rising up from chair, Rudrajeet's eyes darted from one mafia member to another.

"What Devraj saying is true or not?" He demanded answers from them.

The response he got was silence. Every one of them avoiding eye contact, unable to deny the truth.

Their silence broke trust of Rudrajeet. He grabbed his glass and gulped the whole drink in one shot, disgust and dissapointed formed in his expression.

"I've given everything for this partnership. I've helped each one of you grow, protected you when needed, and now, when I need you the most, you're abandoning me?" where is the fucking loyalty?"

In response, Devraj rose from his chair, meeting Rudrajeet's gaze. "We are loyal, that's why we're sincerely informing you about our decision. Koi aur hota toh aapko maarke, aapka business ko capture karleta."

"Also situation is different in here." Devraj continued, unmoved from emotions. "There's no way out of this, if we had way then we could stand with you but we can't! we appreciate and thankful for helping us but...Aap duboge iska matlab yeh nahi ki aapke saath hum bhi doob jaaye, ab yaha koi chutiya nahi hai."

Rachael and Arman chuckle, putting hands on mouth to control their laugh.

Devraj slapped hardly on the table, making them stop to laugh.

Rudrajeet was desperate and anger, exclaimed, "we can stop the police force with our influences, trust me."

Devraj, his expression stern, raised a hand in a halting gesture. "Rudrajeet, if you're planning to start a war with the police, we won't let it happen," he declared firmly. Devraj's hand, signaling an end to their partnership.

Rudrajeet chuckled bitterly, "If you break this partnership, do you think I won't expose your illicit dealings to the world?" His threat hung in the tense air.

Devraj's voice thundered with authority, "If you dare to take such a step, Rudrajeet, the entire underworld will unite against you. Think wisely."

"You all are at my doorstep, I did mistake but I can do it again." Rudrajeet said to Devraj in darkly attitude.

Devraj leaned in, eyes piercing with intensity, "Your threats won't help you now. We're done with you, Rudrajeet."

Rudrajeet glared back. "How are you planning to continue?"

Devraj smirked. "We're not an idiot, we know a lady mafia who is powerful than you. We want to work under her."

"Fine..." Rudrajeet burning with fury, demanded. "Return my 10 crores, each of you borrowed my money for your businesses, I want them back!"

Devraj and the others exchanged glances, reluctantly agreeing, "We'll pay you back soon, but our ties ends now and after paying back. Let's forget each other."

With a gesture, he signaled the others to leave. The members of the once-united syndicate rose, chairs scrapping against the floor, coldly leaving Rudrajeet behind in the room.

☐

Rudrajeet draped in white attire, kneeled before Taniya's photo with a wearied expression etched on his face. Dark circles clung beneath his eyes, revealing sleepless nights he had gone through since her death.

Abhineet and others, their faces reflecting a shared sorrow, stood beside him in respectful silence.

Rudrajeet kissed a flower and delicately placed the flower next to Taniya's photo. "She adored flowers alot," he whispered with broken heart.

"She used to pluck flowers every morning from garden." Abhineet recalled those sweet memories.

"I feel that I failed her...I failed everyone." Rudrajeet still gazing at her photo with tearful eyes.

Abhineet offered a consoling touch to Rudrajeet's shoulder. "You didn't fail her, she knew how much you loved her."

Unexpectedly Abhineet's phone started ringing, he picked up the call. It was the security outside, the security guard's voice resonated through device.

"Someone wishes to enter...his name is Dasya."

Abhineet's gaze shifted from the walkie-talkie to Rudrajeet, seeking permission and guidance.

Rudrajeet's gaze intensified, emotions swirling beneath the surface. The name invoked a complex array of sentiments - dark memories, vengeance, broken promises.

The heavy door of room slid open, catching everyone's attention to the person outside the room and it was Dasya.

Dasya, unafraid, stepped into the room. His face was marred by fresh blood, indicating that he came from gruesome encounter.

He was dressed in black colored suit - covered by blue coat. The symbol of cheetah was designed on left side of coat, same cheetah graced his black tie. Yet some part of suit was stained with blood along with designed cheetah.

Rudrajeet's guards didn't waste any seconds. They raised their guns, pointing them at Dasya's head.

In this intense moment, Rudrajeet stood up and turned around to face Dasya. Their deadly eyes locked into each other.

Dasya glanced at other guards, noticing tension in their faces then he turned his eyes to Rudrajeet again.

Finally, he spoke in his deepened dark voice.

"Nice to meet you, brother-in-law."

To be continued

www.ingramcontent.com/pod-product-compliance
Lightning Source LLC
Chambersburg PA
CBHW070451170726
48291CB00005B/1710